'Tam Linn' (or 'Tam Lin' or 'Tamlane') is one of Scotland's most distinctive fairy tales. It may be best known as a Border ballad, but it has also been retold in many other forms over the centuries. It is mentioned in print as early as 1549, but probably significantly predates this.

THIS BOOK BELONGS TO

_____

_____

_____

My favourite fairy tale, for my favourite heroines and hero:
Mirren, Gowan and Colin — L.D.

To my family, my friends, Xavier and the team and of course,
Jessica – thank you for all your help and support — P.L.

Picture Kelpies is an imprint of Floris Books. First published in 2014 by Floris Books. Text © Lari Don Illustrations © Philip Longson. Lari Don and Philip Longson assert their right under the Copyright, Designs and Patents Act 1988 to be recognised as the Author and Illustrator of this Work. All rights reserved. No part of this book may be reproduced without prior permission of Floris Books, 15 Harrison Gardens, Edinburgh www.florisbooks.co.uk The publisher acknowledges subsidy from Creative Scotland towards the publication of this volume British Library CIP Data available.
ISBN 978-178250-134-3 Printed in Poland

THE TALE OF TAM LINN

RETOLD BY
LARI DON

ILLUSTRATED BY
PHILIP LONGSON

Once upon a time a girl called Janet lived in the Scottish borderlands. Her father was the Laird of Carterhaugh, who owned many fields and hills, and the beautiful Carterhaugh Woods.

Janet was allowed to walk in the fields and on the hills, but she wasn't allowed to walk into the woods.

All the children of the Borders were told the story of a boy called Tam Linn, who had been stolen by the fairies in Carterhaugh Woods. They were told the story of a fierce fairy knight who now guarded the woods for the fairy queen. And they were told *never* to go into the woods.

But Janet didn't believe in fairy stories and Janet didn't like being told what to do. So one bright October day, she crept out of the Laird's house and strode into Carterhaugh Woods.

She walked through the tall trees. She nibbled ripe fruit and listened to tiny birds calling.

She found a stone well with a rose bush growing beside it, and reached out to pick a late flower blooming on a thorny twig.

The stem snapped.

And Janet heard a voice above her: "The fairy queen won't like that."

She looked up.

A young man was sitting in a tree. "The fairy queen doesn't like people stealing fruit or flowers in her woods."

"But these aren't her woods, these are my father's woods. Anyway, I don't believe in the fairy queen or fairy stories."

The young man vanished out of the tree and appeared again standing in front of Janet. "Did you believe that?"

Janet laughed. "Are you a fairy?"

He smiled. "Yes. But I wasn't born a fairy. I was taken in by the fairies when I was a little boy, and I have grown up into a fairy knight."

He stopped smiling and drew his pale silver sword. "You must give that flower back. You must leave these woods and never return."

But Janet held tight to the flower. "Are you Tam Linn? The boy who was stolen in these woods?"

"Yes, I am. How did you know?"

"Because you are still missed. People would be so glad to see you come home."

Janet told Tam Linn that long ago, when his pony trotted back without him, his family searched for him, then wept for him. "All the local children still sing songs about you being stolen by the fairies."

Tam Linn lowered his sword.

Janet asked, "Do you like being a fairy?"

"Of course, because I am magical and powerful here in the woods."

"But aren't you trapped here, working for the fairy queen forever? Wouldn't you like to be human again? Wouldn't you like to leave the woods?"

Tam Linn shrugged. "The fairy queen's magic is too strong for me to break on my own."

"I would help you."

"Why?"

"Because I believe that the boy stolen by the fairies should be allowed to walk back out of the woods."

Tam Linn looked slowly round at the beautiful trees and the shining well, and he nodded. Then he whispered to Janet, telling her how to break the fairy queen's power over him.

Janet promised that she would free him, then left the woods, still carrying the fairy queen's rose.

Once the bright October day had turned to night, Janet slipped away from a Halloween party in the Laird's house. She crept through the woods to the well, and hid beside the rose bush.

At midnight, she heard the fairy queen's army, marching through all the fairy queen's lands on Halloween night.

A fairy knight rode past on a black horse, leading a line of fairy soldiers with bows and arrows. Another fairy knight rode past on a brown horse, leading a line of fairy soldiers with spears. Then Janet saw a white horse approach, ridden by Tam Linn, who had one hand gloved and one hand bare.

Janet remembered Tam Linn's plan and her promise, and she knew that now was her chance to break the fairy queen's power. So she leapt up, grabbed Tam Linn's bare hand and pulled him from his horse.

A voice screeched from high above, "Let him go, girl! He is mine forever."

"NO!" shouted Janet, and she wrapped her arms round Tam Linn, and held him tight.

With one word the fairy queen turned Tam Linn into a snake.
The snake hissed in Janet's face – but she didn't let go.

The fairy queen turned Tam Linn into
a wildcat.

 The wildcat scratched Janet's arms –
but she didn't let go.

The fairy queen turned Tam Linn into a swan.
The swan's wings beat Janet's shoulders –
but she didn't let go.

The fairy queen turned Tam Linn into a stag.
The stag's antlers bruised Janet's ribs –
but she didn't let go.

The fairy queen turned Tam Linn into a wolf.

    The wolf snarled and growled and bit at Janet's sleeves – but she didn't let go.

Finally, the fairy queen turned Tam Linn into a
burning branch.

Janet remembered the plan and the promise,
and Janet knew that she now held all the power.
So she threw the burning branch into the well.

The flame fizzled out.

Tam Linn climbed out of the water, dripping wet and laughing.
The fairy queen screamed as her power over Tam Linn drained away.

Janet and Tam Linn ran out of the woods together.

"Now do you believe in fairy stories?" asked Tam Linn.

"Yes I do." Janet smiled. "Do you believe in happy ever after?"

And so the boy who had been stolen by the fairies, and the girl who resisted the fairy queen, walked towards the Laird's house, leaving the woods behind them.